*To John   P.L.*

*For the children of Greycotes School,
Oxford, who heard it first   S.H.*

HAMISH HAMILTON CHILDREN'S BOOKS

Published by the Penguin Group
27 Wrights Lane, London W8 5TZ, England
Viking Penguin Inc, 40 West 23rd Street, New York, New York 10010, U.S.A.
Penguin Books Australia Ltd, Ringwood, Victoria, Australia
Penguin Books Canada Ltd, 2801 John Street, Markham, Ontario, Canada L3R 1B4
Penguin Books (N.Z.) Ltd, 182–190 Wairau Road, Auckland 10, New Zealand

Penguin Books Ltd, Registered Offices: Harmondsworth, Middlesex, England

First published in Great Britain 1989 by
Hamish Hamilton Children's Books

Text copyright © 1989 by Susan Hill
Illustrations copyright © 1989 by Priscilla Lamont

1 3 5 7 9 10 8 6 4 2

British Library Cataloguing in Publication Data
CIP data for this book is available from the British Library

ISBN 0-241-12526-X

Printed in Italy

# Suzy's Shoes

By Susan Hill
Pictures by Priscilla Lamont

Hamish Hamilton London

In Suzy's room there was a green cupboard.
And inside the green cupboard
were Suzy's shoes.

A pair of shiny yellow wellington boots,

a pair of trainers
with stripey laces,

a pair of old
blue sandals,

and a pair of slippers
with tiger ears.

Suzy liked all of her shoes.
But most of all she liked
taking her shoes OFF!

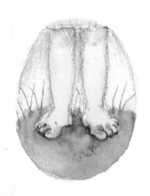  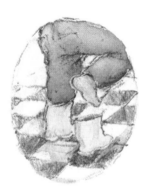 

She took her shoes off

before breakfast,

at the shops,

in the car,

and in the garden.

She took them off

the minute they were all ready to go out

and the minute they got back home again.

A minute too late, sometimes!

And Suzy's father

and her mother

and her big brother Ben

and Mrs Fisher who
looked after her
on Wednesdays

and the lady
at the playgroup

all had to put Suzy's shoes back on.
And then she took them off again.

And everybody said:

"Nobody *else* goes about without shoes on."

"You look silly with bare feet."

"Your feet will get cold."

"Your feet will get wet."

"Everybody else is wearing shoes."

WHAT ELSE
DO YOU THINK
THEYR'E FOR?

PUT YOUR
SHOES ON
SUZY !

THE
GROW
YOU

"Put your shoes on, Suzy.
The Queen is coming!
If you don't put your shoes on
you won't be able to meet her."

So Suzy went to the shop
and got some beautiful shiny new shoes
with bows on.

And she put the shiny shoes on
and she went to meet the Queen.

And she kept her shoes on the whole time.
"Well done, Suzy!
You see, it *is* best to keep your shoes on."

"Isn't it?"